First American edition published 2018 by Gecko Press USA, an imprint of Gecko Press Ltd.
This edition first published 2017 by Gecko Press
PO Box 9335, Wellington 6141, New Zealand
info@geckopress.com

English language edition © Gecko Press Ltd 2017
Translation © Daniel Hahn 2017

Original title: *Loulou*
Text and illustrations by Grégoire Solotareff
© 1989 L'ecole des loisirs, Paris

Distributed in the United States and Canada by Lerner Publishing Group, lernerbooks.com
Distributed in the United Kingdom by Bounce Sales and Marketing, bouncemarketing.co.uk
Distributed in Australia by Scholastic Australia, scholastic.com.au
Distributed in New Zealand by Upstart Distribution, upstartpress.co.nz

Edited by Penelope Todd
Typesetting by Vida & Luke Kelly
Printed in China by Everbest Printing Co Ltd, an accredited ISO 14001 & FSC certified printer

ISBN hardback: 978-1-776571-56-7
ISBN paperback: 978-1-776571-57-4

For more curiously good books, visit geckopress.com

Grégoire Solotareff

WOLFY

Translated by Daniel Hahn

GECKO PRESS

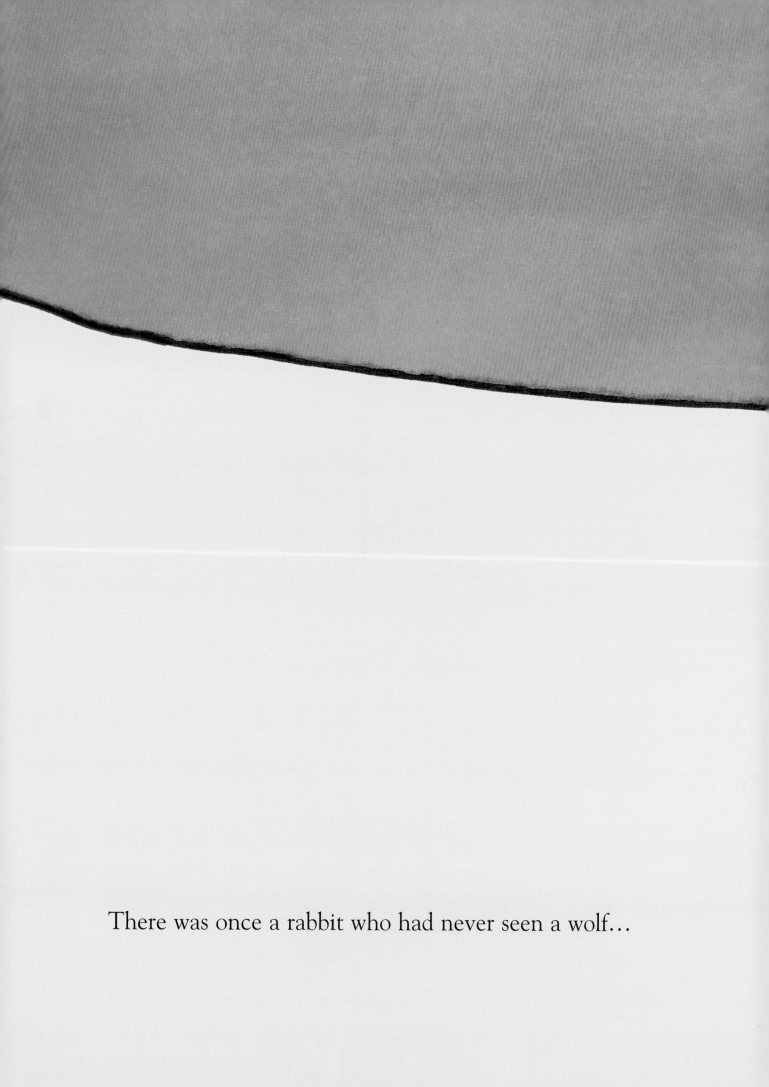

There was once a rabbit who had never seen a wolf…

...and a young wolf who had never seen a rabbit.

The young wolf's uncle decided to take him out for his first ever hunting trip.

But that day, the old wolf was in such a hurry
he crashed into a rock and fell down stone dead.

And so the young wolf found himself all alone.

He was wondering what would become of him
when he heard a noise. It came from a hole
in the ground not far away.

He poked his head into the hole.
A small animal lay in bed, reading a book.

"Hey!" called the wolf. "Can you help me? My uncle
had an accident. He's dead, and I don't know what to do."

"Well, if he's dead," said the small animal, "it's simple:
you have to bury him. I'll help you!" And he jumped out of bed.

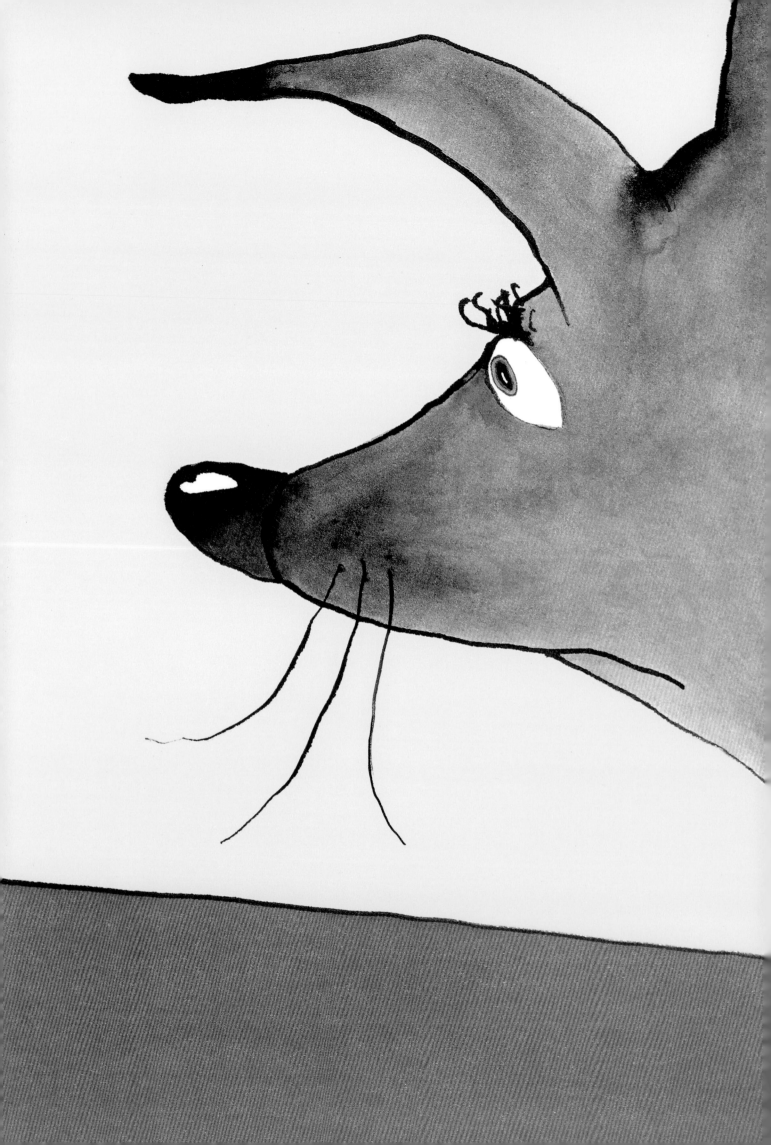

And off they went to the mountain to bury the old wolf.

"Might you, by any chance, be a rabbit?" asked the young wolf.

"Yes," replied the rabbit. "My name's Tom.
And you—are you a wolf?"

"Yes," said the wolf. "But I don't have a name."

"Ah," said the rabbit, "I'm not surprised.
How about I call you Wolfy?"

"Suits me," said the wolf.

"Is it true that wolves eat rabbits?" asked Tom.

"So they say," said Wolfy. "But I've never eaten one."

"Anyway," said Tom, "I'm not afraid of you."

Tom and Wolfy became good friends.
They spent months and months together.
Wolfy grew. Tom taught him to play marbles,
and to read, count and fish for his food.

Wolfy taught Tom how to run really, really fast, much faster than the other rabbits.

Wolfy also taught Tom about being afraid.

Sometimes they played *Who's-afraid-of-the-big-bad-wolf?* and sometimes they played *Who's-afraid-of-the-rabbit?*

But while Wolfy was never afraid when they played *Who's-afraid-of-the-rabbit?* Tom was always very afraid when they played *Who's-afraid-of-the-big-bad-wolf?*

One day, Wolfy scared Tom so badly that the little rabbit rushed into his burrow and decided never to come out again.

Tom spent the whole next day crying on his bed.
It made no difference that Wolfy swore he'd never
eat him, that Tom was his only friend.

No, Tom didn't want to hear it: he stayed in his burrow.

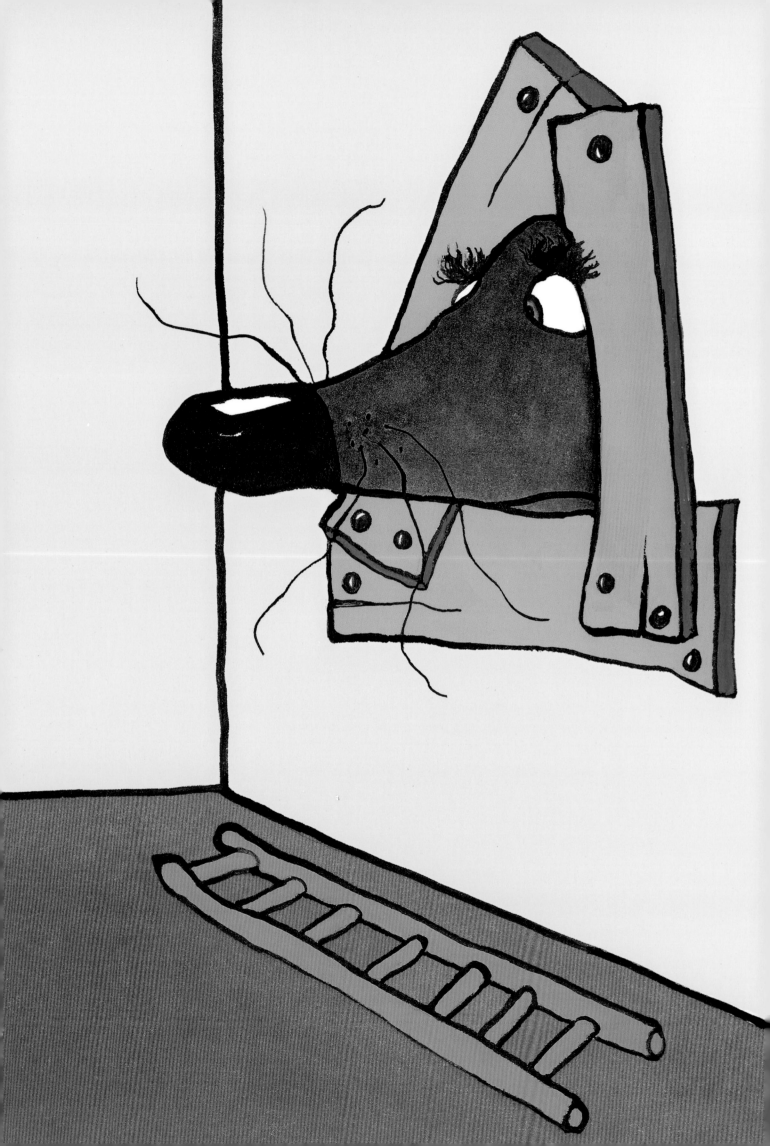

That night, Tom dreamt that Wolfy was huge
and slobbering and gobbling him up!

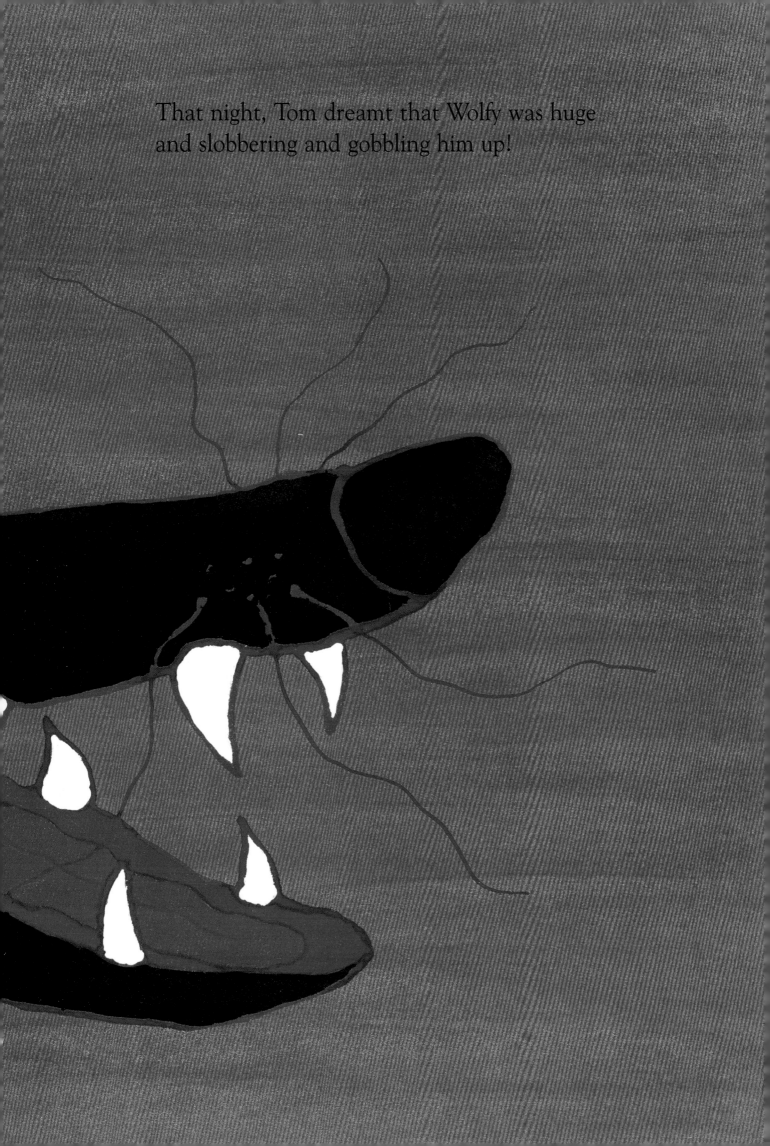

Wolfy thought his friendship with Tom was over for good.

After waiting for several days outside Tom's burrow, he picked up his bundle and set off sadly into the mountains, where he hoped he would find another rabbit friend.

But up on the wolves' mountain, there wasn't
a single rabbit left.

That night, some wolves mistook Wolfy for a rabbit
and chased him over the mountain. He thought
he would die of fear.

All at once, Wolfy understood
Who's-afraid-of-the-big-bad-wolf?

The next day, Wolfy went back to see Tom.

"Tom," he said, "now I understand.
I won't frighten you ever again. I promise!
Come out of your burrow—please, Tom!"

Tom had a think. He said to himself, "If he has been afraid, as afraid as I was, I know he won't do it again."

He came out of his burrow and they threw themselves into each other's arms.

Then off they went fishing, just like before.